# Cowboy Bill

## and the

# Big Umbrella

By ODILLE OUSLEY

Illustrated by FRED IRVIN

Ginn
and
Company

BOSTON     NEW YORK     CHICAGO     ATLANTA
DALLAS     PALO ALTO     TORONTO

Bill had on his cowboy shirt.

He had on his new cowboy boots
and his big cowboy hat.

Bill was going to the cowboy show.

And he was in a hurry.

He wanted to see a real cowboy.

1

"Good-by, Mother," called Bill.

"I am ready now.

I will stop by for Jack and Sam.

They are going to the show too."


But Mother called, "Bill!

Not so fast!  Come here, please!"

"Come back and get this umbrella,"
said Mother.

"I think it is going to rain."

"Oh, Mother," said Bill.

"I don't want that umbrella.

Cowboys don't carry umbrellas.

Not real cowboys!"

3

Bill walked back to the house.

He looked at the big umbrella.

Then he looked at his mother.

Bill did not want to take

the big umbrella.

But he did!

Then he walked slowly away.

"Good-by, Cowboy Bill,"

said Mother.

"Have a good time."

Bill's name was just Bill.

But sometimes his mother

called him Cowboy Bill.

Soon Bill came to Jack's house.
But he did not stop.

Then he came
to Sam's house.
But he did not stop.

He went on
to the cowboy show
with his big umbrella.

Bill went into the theater
all by himself.

He put the big black umbrella
on the floor under a seat.

Then he looked all around.

Can you find Bill here?

Bill saw big girls and little girls.
He saw big boys and little boys.

They had all come to see
the cowboy picture.
They wanted to see
the real cowboy too.

The cowboy picture was funny.

The children laughed and clapped.

Here are some of the pictures
that the children saw.

The children liked the funny cowboy
with the big hat.
They liked his trick pony too.

The children clapped and clapped
when the picture was over.
Bill clapped too.

Then Cowboy Fred came out.

He was a real cowboy.

He played and sang cowboy songs
for the children.

"Zippe-ki-oh-ki-eee!" sang Cowboy Fred.

"Zippe-ki-oh-ki-eee!"

Then Cowboy Fred did tricks.

He did tricks

and more tricks.

Soon the show was over.

Then all the children went out
of the theater.

The big girls
and the little girls hurried out.

The big boys
and the little boys hurried out.


The children wanted to see
Cowboy Fred when he came out.

Soon Cowboy Fred came out of the theater.

He saw the children waiting for him.

Cowboy Fred saw something else too.

He saw the rain.

"What a rain!" said Cowboy Fred.

14

"My car is way down the street,"
said Cowboy Fred.

"Does anyone have an umbrella?"

"Not I," said Jack.

"Not I," said Sam.

"I do! I do!" called Bill.
"I have an umbrella!"

"You don't have an umbrella,"
said Sam.

"Where is your umbrella?" said Jack.

"I'll get it!" said Bill.
"It's in the theater.
I will go and find it.
Wait for me, Cowboy Fred!
Please wait! I will hurry."

"I will help you find it," said Jack.

"I will too!" said Sam.

The boys ran back into the theater.

Bump! Bump! Thump! Up went the seats.

The boys looked under one row of seats.

But the umbrella was not there.

Bump! Bump! Thump! Up went
another row of seats.

But Bill's umbrella was not there.

Thump! Thump! Bump! Up went
another row of seats.

"Hurry! Hurry!" said Sam.
"Cowboy Fred may not wait!"

The boys found a hat and a coat.
They found many other things too.
But there were no umbrellas.

Bump! Bump! Up went another seat
and another.
Then Bill saw something black.

"Here it is!" he called.
Bill picked up the umbrella.
"Come on! Let's hurry!" he said.

The boys ran out of the theater
with the big black umbrella.

"Here it is," called Bill.
"We found my umbrella."

"Good for you!" said Cowboy Fred.
"What a big umbrella that is!"

"Come on," said Bill.

"I will go with you to your car."

The big umbrella was big enough
for Cowboy Fred and Bill.
So away they went.

Down, down came the rain!
Splash! Splash! Splash!

The rain
splashed
on the umbrella.

It did not
splash
on the big hats.

It did not
splash
on the red shirts.

But some rain did splash

on the big boots

and the little boots.

"There's my little red car,"
said Cowboy Fred.
"Thank you for helping me.
What's your name, Cowboy?"

Bill said, "My name is Bill.

But sometimes my mother calls me

Cowboy Bill."

"Thank you, Cowboy Bill,"

said Cowboy Fred.

"Thank you for helping me.

There is nothing like

a big umbrella when it rains."

Then Cowboy Fred took off
his bright yellow kerchief.
He tied it on the big black umbrella.

"Now you have a real cowboy umbrella,"
said Cowboy Fred.
"Good-by, Bill, good-by."

"Thank you, Cowboy Fred," said Bill.
"Come back soon."

Then Bill walked back
to the theater.

He saw Jack and Sam
waiting there.

"Come on, boys," called Bill.
"Come and walk under my
big cowboy umbrella."

So Jack and Sam went with Bill.

They all walked home

under the big cowboy umbrella.

And they sang as they walked,

"Zippe-ki-oh-ki-eee!

Zippe-ki-oh-ki-eee!"

Bill's mother was at home
waiting for him.

"Mother," he called, "Look, Mother.
Just look at my umbrella now!
Look at this yellow kerchief!"

Then Bill told Mother all about
the real cowboy and the big umbrella.

"There is nothing like a big umbrella
when it rains," said Bill.

"You are right, Bill," said his Mother.
"There is nothing like a big umbrella when it rains."
And she tied the bright yellow kerchief
around Bill's neck.